COLD HIGHWAY

SEAN MONAGHAN

COLD HIGHWAY

CHAPTER ONE

The road was very like the kind they would have on television. Was that show even still running?

White and compacted. Thirty feet wide. The long berms five feet high in places, thrown up when the snow was fresh and soft, by the chunky airfoil blade of a snow plough.

Now, those berms were near-rock solid. Packed from the plough, and refrozen overnight.

Cole Wright stood near the back of the canted delivery truck. It was a boxy thing on a GMC chassis. Designed to haul cartons of cookies and cereal, consumer electronics and appliances, fleecy clothing and blankets. Maybe the odd sled or set of skis.

Bigger than a regular UPS van, but smaller than even a rigid semi, the truck fit neatly in that bracket of *no special license required*. Whatever the cutoff was on axle weight restriction before you needed special courses on how to drive.

Still, Wright wouldn't want to drive it out here on the ice. Wouldn't want to back it up anywhere.

He'd done just fine in driver training at the academy. Scraped by one cone on the final test, and finished near the top of the class.

But that was for driving a police cruiser on city streets. Seattle. Some winters they didn't even see snow, and when they did it was never really around for more than a day or two.

Never cold like this.

The truck was painted white, as if it was trying to blend into the surrounds. As if trying to avoid surveillance from the sides or from above. In black lettering along the side--which would be a giveaway--the words *Green & White Haulage* stood almost a foot tall, across two lines. Next to the words was a kind of logo of a stylized truck, leaning forward, with wind lines and tires off the ground, as if it was speeding along.

The road ran on straight to the horizon. The thick pines all around were draped in glorious white snow as if every one was auditioning for the part of Christmas Tree. The sky was clear save for a few contrails. Passenger jets heading from the U.S. to points in Europe. Flying right over the pole.

Passengers all toasty warm at thirty thousand feet, with drinks on demand and little bags of nuts. Leaning back to enjoy a movie on the back of the seat in front.

Wright rubbed his hands together. He had on a pair of *Thinsulated* gloves he'd picked up at a thrift store in Corado, a hundred and fifty miles south. A frozen block of a town that reeked of sawdust and cattle. On a back road that ran off another back road somewhere north of Saskatoon.

Apparently, it was nice in the summer when the days were long and the nights were short. Meadows blossomed with wildflowers and the forests were filled with birds twittering and chirping.

In winter, though, it seemed like the rest of Canada--just a frozen block.

That was unfair. Canada had plenty of things to love. Otherwise, why would he be here?

At the supply store beside the thrift store, he'd bought thermal underwear, thick socks, a thick beanie with a big S machine embroidered on the front, a sweater, a scarf, a jacket and a long coat kind of like a duster.

He was glad of it all, but he was still cold. His breath came out in vaporous tendrils.

And now here he was, looking at a truck with a flat, nosed into the solid berm, just over the brow of a hill, the driver complaining and moaning about the situation, and dark not very far off.

At some point they were going to have to open up the rear doors and start tearing apart the cartons to build a fire.

The driver came around the front. Ron Green, of *Green and White Haulage*. He was well into his fifties, but looked older. His nose was red and his jowls were practically dewlaps. He was carrying probably thirty pounds more than he should be. Liked his beer that was for sure. In these parts it was practically a hobby.

Nice guy. Easy going and ready to take Wright on for just the one run.

"Can't figure you, though," Green had said. "Why anyone would want to go to Stinton this time of year beats me."

"Been baking down in Arizona," Wright had told him. "Needed a change of scene."

"Good man. You can tell me the story on the way up, and we'll hit Icebox Charlie's for a coffee and pizza after, my treat."

"That's real kind of you."

"Me? You're helping me out of a jam here."

And Green had proven a happy listener, somehow able to ask the kinds of questions that kept Wright talking. Wright was used to covering his bases with a minimum of words, minimum of fuss, but Green wasn't taking that. Wanted to know about the state of affairs down in Gollick and points around. The guy had never been farther south than northern Montana. The idea of the sun beating down on you was as foreign to him as a nine to five job or traffic jams.

"You going to help?" he said now, striding from the truck.

Green was dressed better than Wright. A red hand-knitted balaclava that wrapped around his neck and with a face opening that could be pulled right up over his nose. He had exchanged his driving gloves for fur-line mittens before getting out of the cab. His boots were black and thick and clearly waterproof.

"Tell me what to do," Wright said, feeling the cold in his toes. "I'll help all you need."

"Good. I'll give you the winch cable. I need you to take the hook, go up a ways, across the left side of the road. We'll tow ourselves out and get this tire changed."

"Works for me." The truck had a chunky winch set low on the bull bars, the hook tucked back into the grill.

"Glad you're here," Green said. "I can't tell you how often I've been short-staffed and had to make this run on my own. It's been..." He trailed off, head tilted. Listening.

Wright heard it too. Another vehicle. Big. Coming fast up the road from behind.

Hidden by the rise.

Green swore.

"Is this not a good thing?" Wright said. "They can help us."

"They can't see us. That truck'll come roaring over the rise and never be able to stop in time."

Perhaps the truck shouldn't have been painted white, then. Should have been one of those high-vis yellows or oranges. Even that sickly green.

"Come on!" Green said. "Hustle."

He started running back for the rise.

CHAPTER TWO

The approaching vehicle sounded big. A semi. Wright seen a couple coming back the other way as they headed up. Things that looked like they belonged on a freeway rather than hurtling along a narrow ice-covered gravel road.

The drivers got paid by the hour, rather than by the mile. No kind of motivation there to keep their speed down.

As he hurried after Green, one of Wright's boots slipped on one of the ice patches. He threw his arms out. Kept from falling.

His boots were more suited to quiet short hikes along limed pathways during the spring. The place felt like it needed crampons to reliably take a step.

He kept moving, but slower. Green raced on. Clearly confident and balanced. Wasn't that the think with Canadians? They spent more than half their life on ice so it was no problem. Story went that most kids could skate before they could walk.

Wright slowed almost to a stop. They should have gotten out flares. A reflective warning triangle. Something to put back up at the rise to alert oncoming vehicles.

In the road just ahead was a nasty pothole. Two feet across, maybe a foot wide. Five inches deep and filled with churned up slushy ice.

The tire tracks from Green's truck running right through it.

That's what they'd hit that had done in the tire. Made it blow out. Forced the truck into the slewing slide that sent them into the bank.

Wright had to admit, Green had done a good job of keeping them from flipping or spinning right around. Value of experience in driving on ice.

As Wright stepped around the pothole, something in the trees caught his eye. Red. Out of place.

He turned. Stepped closer.

Just the edge of it showing above the high pile of the snow berm.

The roof of a car. Just a tiny corner of it showing. Enough to catch his eye. The rest was coated with snow.

CHAPTER THREE

While they'd rattled their way north, with Green coaxing from Wright details about aircon and cactuses and ground so baked you could pee on it and see it practically dry out before you were done, Green had inserted moments of his own life. Information about the area.

"Economic downturn, let me tell you. Everyone down in Saskatoon and Calgary are living it up on the back of lumber and oil money. Meanwhile everyone up here is living in dirt-floored shacks and paying premium prices for everything."

Wright hadn't mentioned that the mark up on the sodas and nails and other supplies in back of the truck was probably pretty hefty.

The countryside had flown by. Green was a skilled driver.

He pointed out where people lived. Folks who were friends, folks who were standoffish and a couple who were practically blood enemies.

"You think it's the wild west down Arizona way," Green had said--Wright hadn't indicated anything like that--"but up here it can get real vindictive let me tell you. When the nearest cop is an hour or two away, well, sometimes you take things into your own hands."

Wright didn't reply. Had he mentioned that he'd been a cop? Probably not. Not as if he hid the detail, just that if no one asked and it wasn't relevant, he just kept quiet.

Green had thundered along, confident of his skills on the ice, asking questions about iced coffee and what kind of hunting people in Arizona got up to and if people down there even understood snow.

And been surprised when Wright had explained that it did snow in Arizona.

"Up on the plateaus in the north," Wright had said. "Flagstaff and the Grand Canyon. Winters can get bitter."

"Hah!" Green had said, laughing. "You'll never convince me that anyone in Arizona knows the first thing about 'bitter'."

He'd waved his arm at the frozen road and forest around him, and probably needed to give no more explanation.

But that was the moment when they'd hit the pothole.

One hand on the wheel.

Perhaps that's what had made the difference then.

CHAPTER FOUR

The noise of the approaching truck grew louder and louder. The high contrails stretched on silently, and a cool breeze slipped around the trees.

Wright took a step toward the car on the other side of the ice berm.

The car must have gone in before the plough had come through. Before the last heavy fall of snow. The car was tucked into the trees. Some branches stretched down low enough to scrape at the roof. Perhaps it was their movement that had kept that tiny section from becoming snow-covered.

"Hey!" Ron Green called from near the summit of the rise. "What're you gawping at. We got problems here."

Right. A medium-sized truck with a blown tire, dug into the side, with what sounded like a freight-train-sized truck bearing down on it at a hundred. Maybe faster.

Wright stepped away from the car and moved as fast as he could up the rise, following Green.

This side of the rise was maybe a five percent grade, but the other side was steeper. To come up and get over it, Green had kept the truck's speed up somewhere around sixty. That took chutzpah and moxie, really. Confidence in your driving ability.

Lucky that the tire hadn't blown out right at the bottom there on the other side. Coming over, they'd lost maybe half of that speed.

Ahead, Green had come to a stop and was waving his arms back and forth high above his head.

The truck chugged and whined. Still coming fast. Booming sounds accompanied it. The load, shaking and shivering against the bumps from the suspension as the tires ran over the rough ice.

Wright kept moving. He stayed left, on the approaching driver's right. Green was on the same side.

Technically that was correct. Keep to the side of approaching traffic. The driver and you can make eye contact. You don't want traffic coming at you from behind.

But this wasn't a suburban street without sidewalks. Not even some country road with a modicum of traffic.

This was Nowhere, Canada. On their trip so far, they'd encountered one other vehicle coming the other direction. A huge black pickup with double tires at the rear and an array of searchlight-like lenses on a truss across the top of the cab.

They'd skirted past each, delicately, with inches to spare. Stopped for a moment, with windows cracked so the drivers could have a brief exchange about road conditions and what Green was hauling in.

Wright slowed.

The truck was clearly coming fast. Using the same strategy as Green had. Build up speed.

But likewise, the driver would be keeping to the right. To allow as much space as possible on the left to account for that vague possibility of other unsighted traffic coming back the other way.

Which put Green right in the truck's path.

"Hey!" Wright called. "Get off the road. Get up the berm."

Green kept waving.

Wright veered away. Headed for the berm. Started walking along it.

The snow was compacted and frozen just as hard as he'd assumed it would be. It was like walking along the rock riprap on Kennedy River down out of Louisville in Kentucky. Uneven and chunky. He'd been down there months ago, and practically turned an ankle all in the effort to pull a Labrador out of the swirling water.

Green kept waving. Wright was just ten feet from him.

The truck appeared in a rush.

Tips of the high exhausts and the antennas. The little row of orange LEDs strung across the top of the cab's roof.

The windshield. The hood and headlights.

The enormous grill and bull bars that would make a tugboat proud.

The driver gave a blast on the horn.

Green was right in the path.

CHAPTER FIVE

W right leapt forward.
He sprinted. At the edge of the road. Where it met the berm.

His feet crunched in the ice.

Green's arms dropped to his sides. Perhaps he was realizing his situation.

The truck was less than fifty feet off. Coming fast. Brakes hissing. Horn blaring.

Wright grabbed Green's collar. Dragged him away to the left.

The collapsed together. Onto the jagged berm.

The truck blasted by. It brought a wash of oily stink. It was so loud. Racing past. Inches from them.

Wright had jammed his ribs into something. One of the chunks of sticking up ice.

"Ow," Green said.

"You hurt any?"

"No." Green sat up and watched the taillights of the truck rush away along the road. "Could have been killed."

"Thought you would know better, out here."

"Heat of the moment." Green pushed up from the berm. He'd

lost one of his mittens and the balaclava had been pulled back
from his head, revealing thick gray hair and eyebrows.

Wright stood.

The hissing from the truck continued. It was still slowing.

"You did a good job, though," Wright said. "They drove on by
your truck there."

"Did you see it? There was maybe five millimeters in it."

Wright blinked a moment. Canada. Metric. He should be
used to it by now. The road distances were marked in kilometers
and the sodas were marked in milliliters rather than fluid
ounces. Meat was sold by the kilogram.

Five millimeters was, what, a fifth of an inch?

It was a metaphor, anyway, for the truck's load coming real
close.

The truck had come to a stop now, pulled in to the side about
a hundred yards ahead of Green's truck. Yards Wright could do.
Near enough to a meter that you didn't even have to convert. A
thousand yards in a kilometer. Fifteen hundred meters in a mile.

More or less.

Wright stood. Put his hand out to take Green's. Helped him
to his feet.

"I guess," Wright said, "we might be able to skip the winch
here. This guy might haul us out. Maybe."

"Maybe."

They started back along the road.

CHAPTER SIX

Wright spotted Green's missing mitten, lying on the road. The mitten had gone under the big truck's tires and lay crushed into the ice. There were tire tread marks on the fabric.

Green crouched and picked the mitten up, holding it between his thumb and forefinger.

"Gift from my ex," he said. "No real loss."

"You're going to get a cold hand."

Green shrugged. They continued trudging back along the road.

The big truck was hauling a relocatable building. Wider than a regular trailer home, but still, somehow, within limits.

It was beige, with aluminum window frames. The glass was covered in sheets of adhesive paper. Chains and straps kept the building safely on the truck's long tray.

"I'll talk to the driver," Green said. "I'll give you a couple of flares. Go stick them up on the brow of the rise."

"Sure," Wright said. "You got a triangle?"

"A triangle? You mean like that thing that goes 'ping' in an orchestra at just the right moment?" Green looked at Wright and winked.

"That's the one," Wright said. "You're in good humor."

"Well, all is not lost. This guy's come along just at the right moment. Probably saves us a whole lot of work."

They reached Green's truck and he pulled open the driver's door. At the touch of a handle, the seat deck flipped up, revealing a cavity below. Wright glimpsed a first aid kit, some rope and a jumble of other things.

Green took out two long flares and a shiny orange triangle.

"Go join the orchestra," he said, passing them over. "When you're done, head back over and we'll get out of this mess."

The big truck had come to a stop. The door opened and the driver jumped down to the ice.

"Git," Green said.

"Copy that," Wright said, and started off along the road toward the rise again.

Green was like a loveable grump. People would say that he was rough around the edges, but had a heart of gold. *Doesn't suffer fools, but he'd do anything for you.*

At the crest of the rise, Wright set up the triangle. It was a plastic thing made from four flat struts, like school rulers you'd find in any kid's desk. Three of them joined to make the sides, fixed with little bolts, and the fourth was hinged from the middle of one, to make the stand.

Wright stood the triangle just to the left of more or less the center of the road.

He ignited a flare and lay it to the left. Ignited the other. Put it on the right.

The smoke stank and the flames hissed and crackled. The things were going to melt their way through the road.

Wright went to the berm and kicked a one of the protruding blocks. It took him a couple of goes, but the piece of ice broke away. He repeated the kicks on another block and took them back to the flares.

Using the ice, he chocked the burning ends up. The blocks

would probably melt away real quick, but at least he felt like he'd done something.

Turning, he started back.

Green and the driver were standing halfway between the two vehicles, talking. Nothing much else going on.

As he went, Wright edged in toward the berm again. Where he'd seen the red from the car.

He might have been mistaken of course. Some trick of the light. Could have been some piece of reflective tape, maybe, caught in the tree branches. Some piece of debris from a truck, perhaps. Even a child's toy, fallen from someone's trailer and bounced up and over the berm.

Wright stopped again at the pothole. Roads like this, it had to be pretty difficult to keep up with a maintenance schedule.

He clambered up the berm, and right away it was evident that his first assessment had been right.

A car.

As he started down the other side of the berm, Green hollered at him. Wright didn't catch the words, but he turned. Waved.

"Something here," he called back.

"What?"

"Car."

"Leave it. Let's get this done."

"Someone might be in it--"

"It's abandoned. Trust me." Green had walked along to the back of his truck. "Trust me. Happens all the time. They'll come back for it when things thaw."

Right now, it felt as if things would never thaw. Wright's feet were starting to feel like those chunks he'd just kicked off the berm. Little blocks, at the ends of his legs.

"I'll feel better if I check it out," he said.

Green ran his bare hand across his chin. He'd pulled the balaclava back up over his mass of hair.

"Well," he said. "I suppose me and Cheryl here have got this. Don't dawdle."

Cheryl, the truck driver. Wright gave her a nod and a small wave, which she returned.

"Two minutes," Wright said.

He turned and climbed down the rear side of the berm.

CHAPTER SEVEN

I t was a car that he'd seen. No child's toy or piece of debris.
A Toyota station wagon. He saw the emblem, but not
the model name. Older. Perhaps fifteen or more years.
Snow draped it in elegant soft curves, mostly. Save for where the
branches had tapped and brushed away the snow, he never
would have seen it. The car would have looked like just another
hillock.

The snow beyond the berm wasn't as rigid and packed as the
berm itself, but it did still have an ice crust. His boots broke
through with almost no resistance, and dropped into the looser
snow below, compacting it to the ground.

The snow came up to his knees. Dampened his trousers. His
duster draped back across it like a cape. Pieces of the crust broke
away as he walked, like an icebreaker pushing through the
Arctic pack.

Since his feet were numb, he couldn't tell if the moisture was
soaking through to his socks.

Probably.

Once they were on the road again, he was going to need to
take his boots and socks off and press his toes into the truck's
heater grill.

Wright strode on up alongside the car. He brushed the snow from the rear side window. The snow broke away, but left a rime of ice on the glass.

He couldn't see inside, but could tell it was darker. Enough snow lying across the vehicle to cut the light.

He scraped with his fingernails, but didn't make any headway. He took another step. The snow was deeper where it had drifted against the car. Chest height.

There were gaps in the trees ahead of the car, as if they'd been planted in rows, and this one was wider than the others.

Branches trimmed back?

Couldn't be. They weren't here, at the edge of the road.

Wright stuck his arm through crust and the looser snow below fell away easily. He felt around the door, locating the handle. Even with his good gloves, his fingers were growing cold.

Maybe Green was right. The car had been abandoned here and Wright was just wasting time.

Better to get the truck back on the road and sit in the warm cab while they trundled on for Stinton and the little store there expecting cookies and diapers.

Wright felt the handle. He got a grip and pulled. It didn't budge. Locked. Or frozen shut.

He took another step. Reached through the mass of white for the front door handle.

This one moved when he tugged on it.

The latch clicked. Wright pulled some more. The door didn't move much. Up against the mass of snow.

He moved his hand and put in in against the door, feeling for the point where the window frame met the door proper. Both hands. Better leverage.

As he tugged, he heard someone speak from deeper into the trees.

"Hey, mister. What're you doing there?"

CHAPTER EIGHT

Wright was already yanking on the car's door, and it came open with a surprising burst. The snow kind of tinkled and shuffled. It fell away, wrapping itself around the door.

He looked over.

The owner of the voice was wearing a blue and white knitted hat with a pom-pom on the top. Maybe they called it a toorie up here. Something made by a family member most likely. It didn't look store bought.

He had a thick, dark beard and stark blue eyes. A jacket similar to Green's, and gloves about three grades up from Wright's pair.

Across his chest, held in both of those gloves, he had a rifle. Looked like maybe a Marlin, though Wright wasn't too familiar with hunting rifles. It had a lever action below and behind the trigger, and a scope mounted on top.

Didn't matter what kind it was, really, it was the guy's stance. Not threatening, but with the rifle across his chest like that, stock down and muzzle pointed skyward, it was at the ready.

Unlike if it was slung across his back, or held in one hand, muzzle angled down.

The snow came up to his knees. He was wearing waterproof leggings.

"How are you doing?" Wright said.

"Fine. *What* are you doing?"

Wright let go of the door and stepped back a fraction.

"We had a breakdown," Wright said.

"So you figured you'd take the car?"

"Breakdown's under control," Wright said.

From back along the road came the sound of the big truck's engine revving. Green and Cheryl must have gotten the pair hooked up and she was working to pull him out.

"So you're just being a busy-body," the guy said. "A nosey-parker."

"See a car out here buried in snow," Wright said, "I figure that maybe someone needs assistance."

"You're green, huh? If a car's buried in snow, anyone inside is beyond assistance."

"Never hurts."

The guy took a step forward.

Adjusted his grip on the rifle.

Now Wright glanced into the car.

There was someone in it.

Beyond need of assistance, as he'd said.

Only that transition wasn't on account of freezing from the influx of snow over the car.

It was from the bullet hole in her forehead.

CHAPTER NINE

A breeze rattled by. From nearby came the soughing of snow, falling though branches.

Wright stared at the guy with the rifle.

Right there in the snow-covered car lay a woman with a bullet wound in her head.

Bullet wound. Guy with a rifle.

Very easy to do the addition there. One plus one.

The guy stood about ten yards from Wright. Too far off to grab. Not when he was holding a rifle.

They might be unwieldy at close range, compared to a hand gun, but who would take the chance?

The tip of Wright's nose was cold. Growing numb, like his feet. He wasn't doing himself any favors wading around through the drifts like this.

How long did it take for frostbite to set in? He wouldn't even feel it when it did.

Everyone was dressed for the cold better than he was.

Except maybe the woman. He glanced in at her again. The cold wasn't bothering her any.

He scanned the car's interior fast.

There were cracks in the windshield. A bullet hole.

Two.

The snow hadn't penetrated the car. Not much. Except for the clumps that had swirled up when he'd yanked the door open.

Maybe when the fall had first started, little clumps had covered the holes quickly, before much snow made its way inside. Stood to reason.

The bullet holes were tiny.

Two shots.

First one off target. Perhaps deflected by its passage through the glass. Perhaps just a poor shot.

If the car had still been moving, it would have been some kind of marksman to shoot through angled glass and kill the woman.

Although, maybe the car had been parked already. Maybe the shooter was standing as far away as the guy with the pom-pom hat was standing right now.

"Well," the guy said. "Now you've seen it, there's no coming back, is there?"

"Guess not," Wright said. "You see what happened?"

The guy frowned as if it was stupid question. He sniffed. His nose was red. Probably just like Wright's.

"I didn't see it," he said. "But I know who it was."

"Still around?"

"That's the trouble, he is." The guy looked off into the trees. "Somewhere around here."

CHAPTER TEN

W right looked around as the guy had done. Into the trees.

Darkness crept through the forest, turning it dense and black within a few yards. Impossible to see beyond a few of the trunks.

Except for the cleared space ahead.

"Somewhere around here?" Wright said. "What's going on? What actually happened?"

From out on the road came sudden silence. The big truck's engine falling back to idle.

Perhaps they'd extracted Green's truck from where it had been jammed into the berm. Wright hadn't heard any other sounds really. Maybe it was proving more difficult.

"Domestic dispute," the guy said. "He thinks that she should move back in. She thinks that she should head to Calgary and attend university. Psychology or some such. Anthropology? I don't know much about all that."

"Domestic dispute?" Wright said. He could picture it, but it was better to let the talker do the talking. No sense in making assumptions and leading the conversation. Better to echo it.

What those psychologists would call *reflecting*. Not that he was any kind of psychologist.

Just an ex-cop relying in common sense and instinct.

"Should have just stopped there. Kev should have just let her go. Always been his problem. Someone takes and interest and he goes right over the top. The smart ones get out fast. Sarah, well, she was smart, but too kind, in my thinking."

Wright looked at the dead woman again. Sarah.

She looked about twenty-five, though the cold and dry had robbed her of her tone. She looked gray-blue. Her head was angled back and to the side. Her eyes were closed, but her mouth hung open.

She was wearing a thick red woolen coat that ran down across her thighs. She had thin black gloves. One of her hands hung down against the seat, the other rested in her lap.

A thin, glittery layer of frost covered her. A dusting of it.

She'd been steering. Killed, and her hands fell from the wheel. She would have been easing in from the road, coming slow. Foot on the brake.

"You live around here?" Wright asked the guy.

Essentially, though, this was a frozen wasteland. People mostly lived in the small towns, places which serviced the timber and mineral industries.

"Back there a ways," the guy said, with a jerk over his shoulder, rifle barrel indicating something farther from the road. "Got a cabin."

A bird of some kind flew over. Dark plumage, speckled with white. A raptor, perhaps. It gave a piercing cry. Vanished away beyond the trees.

And right then the gap in the trees was obvious. This was an accessway. A narrow road leading in to this guy's cabin.

But covered with snow. No one had been in or out since the car with the dead woman had arrived.

"And Kev?" Wright said.

"Cabin across the other side." The guy indicated ahead, careful to keep the rifle pointed into the sky.

Wright glanced back. There might have been an equivalent gap through the trees there. Another rough right of way.

"But she was turning in this way," Wright said.

"Yeah," the guy said with a sigh. "Yeah, she was.".

CHAPTER ELEVEN

From out on the road, Green hollered for Wright to come help.

"On my way," Wright called back. He took a step away from the snow-bound car. Not toward the road, but toward the guy with the rifle.

"What's your name?" Wright said.

"What's yours?"

"Cole Wright." Wright glanced back toward the road. "We got a flat."

"I figured. I heard the bang. Heard you hit the snow bank."

"Came down to help."

"That was my plan."

Wright waited.

From far off back along the road came the distant sound of another big truck. Busy day.

Green hollered again.

"Looks like your boss is ready to hit the road," the guy said.

Wright waited. Green wouldn't be ready to go yet. He needed Wright's help to get that tire off and the spare fitted. Frozen wheel nuts were going to be a real job there.

"Come help," Wright said. He turned and headed back, pushing through the snow.

After this job, he was going back to the desert. Southern Arizona maybe. Hot and dry sounded real good.

"I guess the cops will be on their way now," the guy said.

"I guess they will be."

"If someone tells them."

Wright stopped and turned to face him. Didn't speak.

The guy stared for a moment. He moved the rifle to his right shoulder and with his left hand, rubbed at his ear. He tugged the pom-pom hat a little lower.

"If someone tells them," he said.

Wright just waited.

"I'd hope they wouldn't," the guy said. "Going to mean problems for me. I like it quiet."

"Hence a cabin in the woods in the back of nowhere in the depths of winter."

"It's not winter yet. Not really."

"What's your name?" Wright said.

"So you can tell the cops?"

"So that I can converse with you like a civilized human being." There would be plenty of people who would argue that living in a cabin out here was nothing like civilized human behavior.

"Hank," the guy said.

"Hi. You want to tell me your involvement here?"

"You a cop?"

"Nope. Used to be though, so maybe I could help you out here."

"What? Like tell me what to say to the cops when they get here?"

"Maybe. I--"

"Wright!" Green shouted from the berm. He was clambering to the crest. "Need your..."

Wright looked around.

Green was staring right at the car with the open door. He had his bare hand tucked into his armpit. Warmer than a pocket maybe. His balaclava was back over his head.

"I think you should get going," Hank said quietly to Wright. "Your boss needs you, and you don't look like you're geared up for the cold at all."

"You're right, I'm not." Wright turned and headed back. He tried to follow the same path as he'd come. No sense in wading through the drifts when he'd already cut a trail.

The cops needed to get out here now. They were probably hours away. And busy enough.

Green had a C.B. radio, but it was busted. Seemed ridiculous, really. Reckless. What if he had a breakdown?

As he had.

There was a phone too, but no service. Why would there be out here?

But Cheryl in the big truck would have a working radio.

"What's going on here?" Green said as Wright came to the base of the berm.

"Don't know yet," Wright said. "It's a real--"

Red droplets sprayed from Green's right shoulder. He tipped forward, collapsing.

The sound of the gunshot caught up.

Echoed through the trees.

CHAPTER TWELVE

Wright moved fast.

He grabbed Green's jacket collar as he fell. Held him up. Stopped him from slamming face forward into the rock-hard berm.

Wright kept moving. He dragged Green as if he was a sack of cut logs. Just making distance. Trying to put space between himself and Hank.

Green's right arm bounced around as if held on just by the fabric of his coat.

Wright followed the berm. What he needed was to get along the trees. Some separation. A barrier.

Green's head lolled.

The ice crunched.

Wright stumbled as he went. His feet collided with heavy chunks of ice.

The shot had come from behind Green.

Hank hadn't been the shooter.

Wright kept moving.

Another weapon.

Kev. That was the obvious answer. Taking exception to people looking over the car.

But the car had been there long enough for him to have done something about it. It was almost as if it had been left there as bait. Maybe Kev just wanted to shoot at anyone who happened by.

The light was fading. Green had said that they'd be in Stinton close to sunset. Still plenty of the day left, but this time of year they were lucky, apparently to get six hours of daylight. And that with an overcast.

The clear sky was a rarity.

Green gasped. He muttered something.

Alive. Good.

Wright didn't have time to stop and check the wound.

There was a first aid kit in the truck. Under the seat, where Green had retrieved the flares and the triangle.

Another gunshot.

Wild? Certainly not in their direction.

Hank shooting back?

The sound echoed.

Wright kept moving. Real hard to keep his balance. Numb feet. Rough ground. Heavy load. Snail's pace.

Head down, Wright kept moving. Berm on his left, trees on his right.

He could slip into the trees, maybe. These guys would be good trackers, if that's what they wanted. But the way Wright was charging around, he'd be as easy to track as a moose in a shopping mall.

"Keep..." Green said. Nothing more.

"Pipe down," Wright said. "We're in trouble here."

Wright stuck his head up. Glimpsed the truck ahead. Over the berm.

He hadn't made as much progress as he'd thought.

Green's truck was still a good thirty yards ahead.

The other truck was still there. Parked another twenty yards on.

Cheryl would have heard the gunshot. She would be on the radio already.

Green was alive. The shot had gone through his shoulder. Pectoral. Bad for sure. Maybe not fatal.

Not a good place to be though. Active shooter.

No back up.

Wright needed to get to Cheryl. She and Green might have gotten Green's truck out from where it had been jammed into the berm, but it still needed the tire changed out.

Wright kept moving. The snow swished around his legs. He was soaked now. From the knees down.

He couldn't keep this up for long.

Hard enough dragging someone along, let alone over rough ground, cold and wet.

If he could get over the berm it would go better. Onto the road. Flat and solid.

Except for the guy with the gun.

"Go..." Green said.

Then the solution appeared. Get the truck. Bring it back. Use it as a barricade.

Wright stopped. He lowered Green to the berm. Tried to nestle him in flat. Head up, feet down against the snow drifts.

Wright pulled Green's balaclava farther down his forehead.

"Back in a minute," Wright said.

"Urg," Green said.

Wright took off.

CHAPTER THIRTEEN

I t took too long. Even without the encumbrance of Green, it was still slow going.

Wright ran as best he could. Sprays of snow and ice crust burst away from his legs.

Ten yards. Twenty.

How long had passed since the shot? Thirty seconds maybe?

He risked bobbing his head up to look over the berm.

Almost at the truck.

Good.

Three more strides. Then he started up the berm. At an angle. Keeping his head down.

Up. Over the top.

Down to the truck.

Cheryl's truck was still parked there. Just where the road was beginning to angle up again. The portable building looked so out of place.

Green's truck was out of the berm, but still leaning down.

The front right tire was wrecked. More than flat. Parts of the sidewall were shredded.

Didn't matter for what Wright wanted.

His heart was pounding. He barely noticed his numb feet. That adrenalin surge was already fading.

Crouching, he glanced back. Green still lay there. Vapor came from his mouth in little puffs. A good sign.

From his angle now, Wright couldn't see the car. No way to see Hank.

The shot had come from across the road. Down that other right of way that matched where Hank had been. A crossroads, but ignored by the main road's snow plough.

These guys would have plough blades on their pickups anyway. Monstrous things. They'd struggle to break through the berm, but then doubtless they had contingencies for that. Spades or dynamite.

Canada.

Wright checked over the berm.

Green's truck was right there. Cheryl's big truck was waiting. No way to tell what she was doing. Wright hadn't even spoken with her.

From the south, beyond the rise. Came the sound of the other approaching truck. Drawing nearer.

Wright's flares were still burning. One had fallen from the ice block and now rested on the road. The reflective triangle still stood. From this distance it looked tiny. Insufficient to bring a huge motoring truck to a stop.

No sign of any people.

Wright scrambled over the berm's crest.

Glimpsed movement to his left.

Gray-white jacket. Similar leggings. Hood.

Rifle.

Pointed directly ahead.

Coming across the road. Heading for the snowbound car.

CHAPTER FOURTEEN

The person in the gray-white outfit was moving slow. Stepping across the road.

Small guy. Maybe five-five. Chunky black boots. Probably rake thin under all that snow gear.

He swung to his right. Sweeping. Looking back toward the triangle and flares.

Wright moved.

Over the berm's crest. Down to the road. He scuttled in front of Green's truck. Warmth still came from the grill.

Still laying out his plans.

Retrieve Green. Get to Cheryl's truck. Get underway to Stinton.

Green's truck was now effective cover. Wright visualized the guy walking across the road. Estimated when it was safe to slide out around to the driver's door.

This was going to take some timing.

Keys.

Surely they were in the ignition.

Maybe that's what Green had been talking about. Wright had heard him murmur 'keep', but maybe that was actually 'keys'.

Trying to give them to him. Maybe they were in Green's coat pocket.

Wright crouched against the bumper. Looked out.

He saw the guy disappearing from view behind the truck.

Wright swung around.

Ripped open the door. Got in.

Keys. Right there in the ignition.

The truck was old, but had seemed pretty reliable. And the engine was still warm.

But it had to start first time.

Wright turned the key.

Nothing.

Not even a starter motor whine.

Again.

Nothing.

He pumped the gas. Foot on the brake. Shifted the transmission to neutral.

Tried the key again.

The engine roared.

CHAPTER FIFTEEN

With the truck's engine starting, right away the fans came on. A blast of luke-warm air raced from the vents.

Wright didn't have time to enjoy it.

He jammed the transmission into R.

Foot off the brake. Hands on the wheel. He jammed down on the gas pedal.

The truck lurched. Bumped.

It wanted to go to the right. The flat right front tire dragging it.

Wright kept his foot down. Hauled the wheel left.

Watched the mirrors.

The guy with the gun showed up. In the reflection.

He'd swung around. Stepped back toward the center of the road.

Wright didn't have to go far.

The truck really didn't want to cooperate, though. It slewed and dragged unpredictably. The wheel had a mind of its own.

The guy raised the rifle.

What Wright wanted to do--put the truck's back right side into the berm--was going to make him exposed on the left.

Couldn't be helped.

He checked the right mirror.

Looked like far enough.

He yanked the wheel hard to the right.

The truck complied too well.

The back end went into the berm. Wright jerked back in the seat. The truck shook. The engine roared.

The front slid around.

Put him almost sideways across the road.

Facing the guy.

Who had his rifle raised.

And it wasn't a guy at all.

It was a woman.

CHAPTER SIXTEEN

The woman still had the rifle raised. She was sighting neatly along the barrel.

Focused.

She'd already shot Green.

But right now, she wasn't aiming at Wright. She was aiming along the road.

But moving slowly back his way.

Wright leaned across the front seats. It was a regular truck set up, with two almost bucket seats for the driver and passenger, with a third, smaller, kind of token seat between for those occasions when a third passenger was required.

There were a few takeout coffee cups and maps and old newspapers piled on it. They rustled as Wright moved across.

He reached for the passenger door.

The rifle fired again. A slightly dulled *crack* doing its best to penetrate the glass.

Not aimed at him.

Aimed along the road.

Wright grabbed the handle. Jerked it. The door thunked.

He swung around. Kicked the door open. Jumped to the road.

He stumbled. Sliding. His numb feet didn't quite work right.

"Arizona," he murmured. "Real soon."

He grabbed the internal door handle. Got his balance.

Moved out from the doorway. Heading back toward Green.

A straightforward set of moves now.

Grab Green. Drag him into the cab. Drive up alongside Cheryl's truck. Transfer Green. Get out of Dodge.

Except that as he took the first stride from the truck, he saw what the woman had been shooting at.

Cheryl.

Lying on the roadway. Sprawled out.

Another rifle lying near her.

CHAPTER SEVENTEEN

W right stepped forward. Following the edge of the truck's boxy cargo compartment. The sign loomed over him. *Green and White Haulage.*

Wright kneeled. Lay forward on the ice. Looked under the truck.

A knobby rime of dirty ice coated the steel, all along the chassis and tubes and axles. The exhaust system was the cleanest part.

The woman's feet were about ten yards back. Walking forward. The chunky black boots firm on the ice with each step.

She was heading around the front of the truck he'd just backed into the berm. Heading for Cheryl.

The woman wasn't interested in Wright.

But why had she shot Green?

Wright pushed himself up. Tiny chunks of ice fell from his coat and duster and trousers. They pattered to the road's surface.

Much more of this and he was going to freeze to death.

He made for the berm. Clambered over.

Green was about three yards along to his left. Even with struggling to steer the truck, Wright had still managed to get pretty close.

Except he was in the wrong place now. With the woman coming forward, he couldn't go back to the passenger's side. She would see him right away.

Best practice, he knew, was to keep away from the crazy person with the gun.

Wright scrambled down. Green was still breathing. His eyes were glassy.

"Hang in there," Wright said.

Green made no reply.

"Sorry about this." Wright grabbed Green's collar again. Dragged him back through their own tracks following the wrong side of the berm. Wright looked ahead for any sign of Hank.

Maybe the woman had been aiming for him, rather than Green. Maybe she was a bad shot. Who wouldn't be in this kind of cold?

She had managed to gun down Cheryl, though.

Wright came parallel with the side of the truck. He popped his head up and checked.

No sign of the woman.

Smart thing to do would be to wait for her to show in front of the truck. Then he could go around the back. Head directly for the driver's door.

Except that she would have known what he'd done, slipping out from the cab. She might have gone around the left side of the truck, ready to surprise him.

This was a very mobile situation. Changing real quick.

All in the space what, three minutes? Wright had just now been talking with that guy Hank about the dead woman in the car.

Wright waited.

Getting into the trees might be the best option right now. He was unarmed. Unable to defend himself in the situation.

Key thing, though, was getting Green some help.

Another gunshot echoed around.

It had come from ahead. From his left. In the trees.

Toward the snowbound car.

Was that Hank shooting back?

Didn't matter.

The thing was, Wright was heading in the wrong direction now.

Toward the shooting.

CHAPTER EIGHTEEN

Back in Seattle, years ago, Wright had been part of a standoff. An estranged ex-husband had shown up in Aston Downs with a rifle. Shot up the house. Sworn he would kill his former wife, and her new boyfriend, and their child, if he didn't get the visitation rights to his own child.

Ten patrol cars, S.W.A.T., a helicopter. Police negotiator in place, shouting through a megaphone at first, in what was usually a quiet neighborhood, then on the phone.

Fall leaves had swarmed around, gathering in the gutters and piling against tires. Wright and the other officers had worked on securing the neighboring houses, evacuating or sheltering in place. Wright had personally escorted a pregnant woman out through a back yard onto the neighboring street where an ambulance had come around to take her to the delivery suite.

It was all very precise and orderly. Improvising, but still with a set plan. The cars parked in a particular way. The negotiator stationed in the correct location. Step by step, with some flexibility, but still from a standard checklist.

A checklist which got revised after the outcome, the guy dead and the woman left with a traumatized child, a boyfriend who broke up with her on the spot, and a house full of bullet holes.

Wright had no checklist for this. People shooting at each other on a frozen Canadian road. Every step was improvising.

He needed to get Green safely to medical care. Fast.

Needed a bandage immediately.

Needed to get aboard Cheryl's truck. For her to take them north to Stinton while Wright did what he could to stabilize Green.

Minutes counted.

And Cheryl was dead.

Wright had never driven anything that big.

Ahead, through the trees, he caught a glimpse of movement.

Hank?

Had to be.

Wright stopped. Crouched.

Beside him, Green wheezed. Time was important here.

The shooting had stopped.

Green needed help.

"Wait here," Wright said.

He began scrambling up the berm.

CHAPTER NINETEEN

The sound of the next approaching truck was growing. It sounded at least as big as Cheryl's. Some big piece of equipment getting freighted north, with the huge kind of rig required to pull it.

Wright moved fast. He reached the top of the berm right in behind Green's little truck. Backed in hard from where Wright had just slewed it in. The double doors at the back of the cargo bay were now virtually parallel to the road.

Wright jumped from the crest of the berm. Grabbed to the top edge of the truck.

The truck's tires were still down on the roadway, but the back end was jammed into the high berm. That got him halfway up straight away. With momentum and his jump, he was just about able to vault up with his hands on the truck.

Not quite.

Cold muscles. Numb feet.

His thighs caught the edge. Wright fell forward. Landed with a thump on the truck's roof.

The cargo compartment boomed. Loud.

Quieter than a gunshot, but still. A dead giveaway.

Wright hauled himself across. The layer of frost on the

aluminum skin rasped under his clothing. Sucked heat from him.

He kept moving.

Right away he could see it was an ill-formed plan. Clamber over the truck, drop to the ground, grab the first aid kit, get back to Green.

Ill-formed since Wright didn't know where the shooters were now.

With all the noise he'd made getting up here, though, they knew where he was.

Wright kept moving. He'd started now. Had to see it through.

He reached the forward edge of the cargo compartment. Right above the cab.

Wright lifted his head. Looked right.

Cheryl's truck stood there, with the portable building on the back.

Cheryl still lay on the road. Sprawled out. There might have been some blood around her. Hard to tell in the against the dirty colors through road's ice surface.

No sign of the woman.

Wright looked left.

The flares were still burning. The triangle was still standing.

No sign of the woman.

But there was Hank. Prone on the berm. Lying out like a sniper. Sighting along his rifle.

Hank lifted his head. Waved to Wright.

As if they were buddies. In this together.

At the moment, Wright knew that Green had been shot. Looked like it had been the woman.

Hank was making some kind of signal with his arm. A closed fist. He shook it twice to his left. Then held the same hand up, with two fingers raised. Then, with one finger, pointed toward Green's truck.

It meant nothing to Wright. Nothing like any signal systems

he'd tried to learn back in the day. Wait. Wait two minutes. Go ahead. Go fast now!

Wright moved back. He was less worried about Hank than he was about the woman. But Hank still had a rifle. Too easy to get shot in that situation.

Two people already had.

Hank dropped his hand. He ducked again. Sighted along the rifle.

Low. As if aiming under Green's truck.

Under.

Was the woman on the other side? The right.

If Wright dropped down onto the left, he might just make it.

And might just get caught in the crossfire.

Wright moved.

CHAPTER TWENTY

Wright slithered forward across the front edge of the truck's cargo compartment. He swung around. Dropped his feet to the cab's roof.

The metal boomed.

Not as loud as the compartment had when he'd landed on that, but still pretty obvious.

His feet slipped. The cab's roof was slicker than the compartment's. The cab was kept warmer. Perhaps ice hadn't formed.

Wright found himself skidding back. He dropped to his knees. Had a moment of regret as he headed backward over the edge.

He whirled his arms. Managed to keep from tipping.

But didn't arrest his momentum.

He dropped off the edge. Slid past the windshield. Collected one of the wipers as he went. Ripped it off.

He landed heavily. His numb feet suddenly became alive with electricity. Already abused nerves firing off in complaint.

He tumbled over and landed on his back. Just about had the wind knocked from him.

The woman appeared from around the right side.

She had the rifle in both hands.
Aimed down.
Aimed at him.

CHAPTER TWENTY-ONE

Under the back of Wright's head, the road was cold and hard. In summer, chances were it was way softer. Muddy or dusty. The trees would be ice-free and shining green in bright sun. The days would be long and warm-ish, and birds would chatter from the branches.

But now, none of that. Solid road. Trees hidden away under ice. The birds all gone south. The sky clear, but darkening.

And a woman standing over him with a rifle. Although, that kind of thing wasn't seasonal.

She stood about five feet back from him. Out of reach.

Both hands on the rifle. The barrel aimed square at his chest.

"Hey," Wright said. He figured the angles. The nose of the truck was between her and where Hank was lying.

If he was going to shoot her, he was in the wrong place.

No way he could have shot her under the truck anyway.

"My friend's hurt," Wright said. "I was trying to get the first aid kit. From the truck."

"It was on the roof?" she said.

"People were shooting. Figured I was more useful to him if I stayed out of the line of fire."

"Smart thinking. Except that now, you're in the line of fire."

"Looks that way. But you don't have any beef with me."

"Maybe I just don't like the way you look."

"You wouldn't be the first." Keep them talking. If they're talking, they're not shooting.

"Are you trying to be funny?" she said.

"Absolutely not. I'm told that I have sense of humor. That I should avoid jokes on pain of death."

"Yeah. You should."

"I'm Wright," he said. "Cole Wright. I'm just along for the ride here. Delivering groceries."

"Groceries?"

"Yes."

"I figured you for a recovery crew. Come to take Sarah out of here. Maybe the car."

"Nope. We blew a tire. That was all. Trying to--"

The woman jerked the gun up.

Stepped back.

Fired. Blind first.

Then aiming.

Fired again.

Worked the action. Ejected the shell. Fired again.

Back toward where Hank had been.

Wright rolled. Scrambled up.

He dove forward.

Tackled her.

CHAPTER TWENTY-TWO

Wright's tackle was a thing of magnificence. It would have made any linebacker proud. A quarterback sacking. A receiver crushed taking the ball five yards from the end zone.

Maybe it should be a hockey analogy. A forward slamming back into the Perspex wall. What were the positions in hockey anyway? They all seemed to just mix up all the time, like vegetables in a stew.

The woman went down with Wright's shoulders against her hips.

She fired again. Wild. High into the air.

Then they were on the ground.

She landed hard. Yelped.

Her hip bone jabbed Wright's clavicle. She smelled of lavender, as if she'd put on some kind of scent before heading out on her killing spree.

Wright's numb feet bounced around, like bowling balls on the end of a tether.

The woman squirmed. As long as he was close, she couldn't shoot him. Not with the rifle.

She was small. Little more than five feet. Maybe a hundred pounds. Hundred ten. Wiry and lithe.

She kept squirming. Slipped from his grip. An oiled eel.

Wright grabbed at her clothing, but his fingers were stiff and kind of unresponsive. Not as numb as his feet, but still not working right. He couldn't get a grip.

Then she was gone. Up and away.

Wright swung around. Leapt to his feet.

She was running.

Heading for the blocked vague right of way across from Sarah and the car.

The rifle lay on the road. The strap was draped across the rifle's stock.

Wright took a step toward it.

Crime scene.

Standard practice was just leave everything as you found it.

Except that she was slowing now. And she had another weapon out. A little black handgun. Some kind of pistol.

Wright swept forward. Grabbed the rifle's strap. Kept moving. Right across toward the other side of the road.

Another sound now.

The other truck. Down shifting, but close. Right there on the other side of the rise? Coming up the steep side.

And Hank was lying there on the road. Halfway between the flares and triangle, and Green's truck.

Face down. His own rifle still in his hand.

The back of his head was missing. Just a crater there.

Fool. He'd moved. Come right into her line of fire.

The new truck gave a blast on its horn. Almost at the crest of the rise.

The woman was still moving, but she slowed. Across the road now. Heading toward the berm on the far side. Heading for that gap through the trees.

The other truck began appearing, just the way that Cheryl's

had. Top of the trailer. Exhausts. Lights across the cab's roof. Windshield. Grill.

The woman raced away up onto the berm. Real fast. Lithe and springy. Athletic.

Gone.

And here came the truck. The driver staring straight ahead. Extra observant because of the warnings Wright had put in place atop the rise.

Wright standing there holding the rifle.

With a body in front of him.

Another behind.

CHAPTER TWENTY-THREE

The truck had a big bulldog right in the center of the front of the hood. Mack.

The brakes hissed and the engine growled. Wright could practically feel the hot air rolling back from the engine. The stink of the exhaust caught up, like a forest fire nearby.

Wright kept a hold of the rifle.

It might take a lot of talking and a lot of explanation later. He might have to call in some old favors.

Right now, though, it wouldn't look good.

Holding a rifle that any moron could tell had been used in the shooting. They wouldn't even need ballistics. Who else was out here?

Not the woman. She was ghost now. Vanishing into the forest.

The truck was still moving fast. It shuddered. On the back it had some kind of tank. Water or sewage. It was blue. Looked like that kind of heavy plastic from a huge rotational mold. Wider than the truck. Ten feet across, and ten feet high. It had a conical top with a low slope, and some kind of hatch on the top. Straps and chains held it down, the same way as the building on the back of Cheryl's truck.

The new truck jerked and hissed. The hood shook and the whole cab moved independently of chassis. Big springs in there. Or air shocks or something.

Wright tossed the rifle aside. Right back in the same spot.

He raised his hands. Walked to his left. Toward the other berm.

He stayed facing the new arrival, but kept his head cocked toward the position where the woman had vanished. She could be hidden in the trees there. Could be drawing a bead on him with that pistol.

Pistols weren't great over distance. Not like a rifle. But she'd already proven she was a reasonable shot. Maybe she had another weapon there. Maybe a whole cache.

It would be better if he could be on the other side of the new truck. Keep it between himself and her.

But he needed the driver to be able to see him. See him clearly.

It was still slowing. Was coming up on passing him. The front tires were going to go either side of the woman's rifle.

Wright took a step up on to the berm. It was just as hard and rough as the one on the other side.

He was aching now. The cold. Landing badly. Tackling the woman. Any linebacker would be mocking him. If it saved the game, maybe it was all right to get hurt, but any other time, you needed to be able to get up and get right back into the game.

And Wright's tackle hadn't saved the game. Not even close.

Made it worse if anything. For himself. For Green.

The driver stared at Wright as the truck eased on by. The panels were painted metallic red, and words on the door read *Big Pine Tanks*. The logo was a vague cylinder with a pine tree growing from the top.

Then the cab had gone on by. The little bunk space in back. The tools and equipment. The front of the trailer. All just a few feet from Wright's face.

There wasn't just one tank. Of course. There were three.

Spaced out along the fifty foot length of the trailer, with pallets in between, stacked with boxes and equipment bound up in plastic sheeting. Everything had a thin coating of ice.

The guy could keep on moving if he wanted. Head on up to Stinton and tell them what he'd seen.

Real mess, he could tell them, *guns and bodies and a truck backed into the berm.*

But he didn't keep going.

The brakes gave a final hiss and the truck shuddered. The tires slid a little on the ice.

Wright dropped his hands.

The truck made more sounds. Gurgling of fluids and the clanks of mechanisms battling each other.

The driver's door opened and a heavyset guy in a sleeveless jacket swung around and balanced himself on the top step.

He was holding a silver revolver.

He had it pointed squarely at Wright.

CHAPTER TWENTY-FOUR

The metallic red truck's engine burbled, idling against the cold. Frost stuck to the panels in the cooler spots. The driver had a thick, scruffy beard. Kind of guy who'd worked to earn the right for a thick beard.

The truck was parked on the right. Green's truck was hidden now, but on the other side.

The road was blocked. Chances were, though, it had seen all the traffic that it would until tomorrow.

The revolver was a Smith and Wesson. Silver plated, with bone grips, from the little Wright could see of it. The kind of thing that the driver would keep in his glove compartment for occasional moments such as this.

The barrel looked huge. Six inches of it. A hand gun, but doubtless the guy could hit him from here. A barrel like that made it even more accurate.

Maybe he'd even spent some time at a range and fired of a whole lot of rounds and gotten used to the feel and the weight of it. Targets at ranges could be a whole lot farther off than Wright was now.

"Looks like there were some problems here," the guy said. He had a soft voice. The kind of vocalization you might expect from a radio weather reporter. Trustworthy.

"Yes sir," Wright said. "Problems for sure."

The guy nodded. Glanced away along the road. Cheryl lay maybe thirty yards from the nose of his truck.

"Care to explain?" he said, looking around at Wright again.

"Long story." Wright kept his hands up. Just at shoulder level.

The driver stared at him. Waiting. The gun stayed level. Not held out. The driver kept his elbow in at his side. Not a real shooting stance, but that wouldn't matter to the bullet.

"We had a blowout," Wright said. And he explained about seeing the car, about Hank, about Cheryl stopping her truck. On through Green's shooting, moving Green's truck, and Wright's tussle with the woman.

"She ran off," Wright said. "She still has a gun."

"Pretty good story, buddy," the driver said.

"You have a radio?" Wright said. "C.B.?"

The driver frowned. "Of course I've got a radio."

"Call it in. Please. I'm going to help my friend." Wright dropped his hands and started along the berm. Heading for the front of the red truck.

"Hold up," the guy said.

"My friend is bleeding out," Wright said.

"I can't let you go."

"I had the rifle, huh?"

"I saw you, plain as day as I came up over the hill."

"It's under your truck now."

"There's another one. I saw that."

Hank's gun. Still in his hand where he'd fallen.

Wright needed to check the others too. Cheryl and Hank.

But he knew that Green was alive. Triage, in effect.

"Come with," Wright said. "I could use your help. You can keep me covered. Go check on the other two. But I need to go help my friend."

The driver ran his free hand across his mouth. Considering.

"All right," he said. "I'm Silver. Paul Silver."

"Cole Wright."

"Pleasure. I'll be right with you. Let me get my first aid satchel."

He set the revolver back on his seat and climbed over it.

Wright didn't wait.

CHAPTER TWENTY-FIVE

Green was still breathing. His skin was pale. He was shivering.

He stared at Wright, bleak and scared. As if he could feel his life slipping away.

"We'll get you taken care of," Wright said.

"Urg," Green said.

Wright had grabbed the first aid kit from Green's truck. He worked fast. Unzipped Green's jacket. Ripped open his blood-soaked shirt, spilling buttons.

Running on adrenalin now. The cold was seeping into Wright's bones now. Into his core.

Could he get hypothermia when he was running around so much?

"This one's breathing," Si, the red truck's driver, called from over the berm. "Grazed, that's all. Bumped his head pretty good falling on the road from the looks."

"Good news," Wright called back. "Can you get him some-where warm?"

"Ahead of you there."

Wright lifted his head and saw Si's head come up. Hank draped across his shoulders.

Wright turned back to Green. Pulled back clothing. Cut away his thermal undershirt. It might have been red in the first place, but now it was blackened and darker with blood. It stuck to his skin.

The wound was a mess. Ragged and bloody. Pieces of bone in it.

Way less blood than Wright had expected, but then Green was running low on that.

From the kit Wright got a saline bottle. He irrigated the ruin of Green's shoulder. Green winced.

Wright got a flat pad. He ripped open the packaging and placed it over the wound. Put another one crosswise. Taped them both down.

He rolled Green.

The entry wound was better. Oozing blood, but smaller. Wright put another pad over it. Tape. Then he got a crepe bandage and did his best to bind around the shoulder, running under his armpit and up close to his neck.

"You should shower more," Wright said. That armpit was the stuff of nightmares.

"Had one..." Green said, wheezy. "Just... last week." He even managed a smile.

"Come on," Wright said. "Let's get you into the truck."

As he lifted Green, Wright heard the truck's engine rev higher. Coming up from idle.

Silver was getting impatient.

Good. There was no time to lose.

Wright hustled. He'd done the best he could. Now they needed to get these people to real help.

As he reached the top of the berm, though, he saw the truck pulling away. It hissed and graunched.

Picked up speed fast.

The tanks rumbled on the load bed.

"Wait," Wright said. But it was useless. The truck picked up speed quickly.

Carrying Green, Wright moved along the side of Green's truck. With numb feet, it was all Wright could do to stay upright.

The red truck was gone. It left behind the woman's rifle, lying there on the road.

And Silver and Hank.

"She took it," Silver said. "She just took my truck."

CHAPTER TWENTY-SIX

Wright stood watching the departing truck. Stolen by the woman who'd shot Hank and Green.

Wright might have given chase. Except for the two wounded men. They needed to get them to medical care. Real fast.

And maybe Cheryl, the other driver too.

If she was still alive.

There was another truck. Cheryl's.

The red truck was just pulling alongside it. Easing along the left of Chery's truck. Real close.

"She's going to wreck my truck there," the driver said. "She's too small to be driving something like that."

As if prophetic, one of the straps holding the rear tank in place caught on the trailing top corner of the portable building.

Silver swore.

The trucks jerked.

The woman kept driving. If anything, she pushed harder.

The engine roared.

The tank made a deep booming complaint. The sound echoed through the trees.

Tires began sliding.

Silver started after her.

The back end of Cheryl's truck shifted around. Tugged to the left.

Something snapped in the building. One of the glass panes shattered, held together by the adhesive paper covering.

The woman kept driving. Ice tires, but no chains. Not necessary on a solidly frozen road.

But she wouldn't be able to keep going for long.

Silver kept running. Confident on the ice. Wright wouldn't dare not with ice block feet.

The portable building made more breaking sounds. Snapping and bending.

Then the strap on the tank gave way.

It made a sound like a plucked bass guitar. The deepest string.

The tank jerked. But there were still other straps holding it in place.

But then the portable building rocked away to the right. As if sagging on its foundations.

The tank rocked to the left.

And both of them rocked back together.

Without the impediment of the strap tugging and holding the truck back, the tires got new bite and the engine was freed.

Which seemed to swing the tank faster.

It collided with the side of the returning building.

The sound was extraordinary. Loud. Booming and splintering. Together with the twanging of various straps giving way.

The tank tipped back off the truck's trailer. Landed on the berm. Sideways.

The tank began rolling backward. Away from the trucks.

Toward Wright and Silver, Green and Hank.

Silver swore.

CHAPTER TWENTY-SEVEN

The engine on Silver's truck revved hard. When the tank had tipped off the trailer, the weight had shunted the trailer sideways. In and under the trailer on Cheryl's truck.

Cheryl. Whose body was still lying on the road.

In the path of the approaching tank.

Wright blinked a moment.

It was like something out of a kid's television cartoon. The coyote tips a boulder at the bird, but then the boulder rolls right back toward him.

The tank was coming slowly, but picking up speed. Rolling off the berm and the trailer.

"That thing weighs over half a ton," Silver said.

"Get back up off the road," Wright said.

It was like a being a pin in a bowling alley with the side rail barriers up over the gutters so that the little kids would always knock something down. The tank would bounce back and forth off the berms and stay right along the middle.

Wright headed toward Cheryl's body.

Probably dead, but then bad enough for her family that she was dead without her body being flattened like roadkill.

And if she was still alive, she wouldn't survive being run over by that thing.

The tank had one edge on the truck's trailer, and the other edge on the berm.

Wright's feet felt huge. His legs were slow. He'd been running around in this diabolical cold for too long now.

Moving too slow.

Thirty yards from Cheryl. The tank was another fifty yards beyond her.

He tried to pick up speed, but there was nothing left.

He just kept going.

The tank bumped as it rolled. Ice along the berm crushed away under it. Perhaps it wouldn't be like a bowling alley at all. The tank might just curve away and break through the berm, knock down a couple trees and just come to rest.

Twenty yards to Cheryl.

The tank came off the back of the trailer and right away picked up speed.

Somehow the little bit of slope had been enough to get it going.

Forty yards beyond Cheryl.

The tank made terrible otherworldly sounds. Submarine sounds. Booming and deep rattling.

It was rolling slightly uphill now. Still coming.

Thirty yards from Cheryl.

Wright was ten yards from her.

The tank slewed and shifted as if it was struggling to decide the best path to take.

Twenty yards.

Wright was still five yards from her.

The tank loomed. Black and solid.

Ten yards.

Wright reached Cheryl.

The tank continued to bear down on him.

Left or right?

Toss of a coin.

Wright grabbed her collar. Same way that he'd hauled Green along at first.

Three yards.

He was reminded of a movie he'd seen once. A giant horse-shoe of a crashing alien spaceship had slammed down near a couple of survivors, and had begun rolling toward them. They had to choose left or right too.

Wright just went to his left. Dragged Cheryl along.

One step. Two.

And he dove ahead. Aiming for the berm. Did what he could to toss her ahead.

The tank trundled on by. Less than a yard away.

And kept moving. Booming and shuddering. It crushed Cheryl's rifle.

"You okay there?" Silver called. He was up on the berm too, back near Green's truck. Both Hank and Green were nowhere in sight. Had he brought them over the berm with him?

"We made it," Wright said.

The tank was still moving. Slowing as it crept up the shallow incline.

Farther on, the flares still burned and the triangle still stood.

Wright turned to check Cheryl.

Her mouth hung open and her eyes were glazed. She wasn't breathing at all, and her coat had some blood splatter.

The wound was on her neck. A chunk torn from it.

She'd been dead before she'd even hit the ground. She'd hardly bled at all.

Still, she wasn't flat.

From up toward Silver came a crunk sound, and a shattering of glass.

Wright looked over and saw that the tank had tapped Green's truck.

Solidly. The cab was partway crushed, right over the passenger seat. The cargo compartment had been broken too. The panels snapped away from the corner joins.

And the tank was now rolling its way back down.

Toward Wright, and Cheryl's body.

CHAPTER TWENTY-EIGHT

Wright moved fast. No idea where he got the energy. He hauled Cheryl up over the berm and into the trees. Left her behind a trunk. Icy snow rained on him as he jostled through the branches.

The sound was lost in the rumbling of the tank.

The poor cops were going to have a terrible time when they did get up here. This had to be one of the worst crime scenes he'd ever seen. And he'd done a fair job of contaminating it himself.

Wright scrambled back to the top of the berm. The tank was picking up speed. At least it was traveling too obliquely to roll over the berm.

Ahead, Silver's red truck was jammed in against Cheryl's. The portable building had fallen onto Silver's trailer and was holding the pair together. Jammed in on the middle tank and the pallet of other supplies.

The woman kept revving the engine hard. The cab unit shook and rocked as the vehicle tried to drag its way ahead.

Wright waited for the tank to roll by. The sound was terrible. Booming and shuddering over the ice. When he dropped from the berm to the road, he could feel the shaking, like little earthquakes.

"Wait here," he called back to Silver.

"Not going anywhere," Silver said.

The tank was moving slower than walking pace, but picking up speed.

Wright kept moving. The tank angled left, as if it was planning to remount the trailer so that everyone could get on their way.

Wright crossed. Headed along the road, just at the right hand berm.

The tank kept picking up speed. If it could, it would just roll on all the way to Stinton by itself.

Except for the hills and corners.

And the two trucks parked blocking the road now.

Wright's feet ached. He probably preferred them numb. As he ran, his nerves kept shooting jabs of electricity at him. Like pins and needles, just ten times worse.

The woman was still revving the truck's engine. Still trying to get herself out of the situation.

As Wright approached, the engine sound changed. The truck shook. Backed up a little.

The portable building creaked. Straps twanged.

She revved some more. Still in reverse.

Still jammed in.

The tank she'd lost kept rolling. It struck the back of the trailer hard. Made the truck shake. The tank boomed again. A final time as it came to rest. Wasn't going anywhere now.

Wright edged along the right hand side of Silver's truck. He'd parked really close to the berm. Good practice, really. Leaving as much of the road clear as possible.

The building was a ruin. Whoever had bought was going to be pretty unhappy.

Wright was still working on how he was going to figure this one out. He didn't want to go along the left and show up in the truck's mirrors. But from this side, he would have to go around the front of her.

If the truck broke free, chances were it would lurch forward and collect him on the way.

All he needed was her out of the way so that he could load Hank and Green into the back of Cheryl's truck. Silver could drive them to Stinton.

They'd have to unhitch the trailer, which would take time, but they'd easily make that up on the road without having to haul the destroyed building.

Then it was obvious.

Through the cab on Cheryl's truck.

CHAPTER TWENTY-NINE

The racket of the engine on Silver's truck died back. Right down to an idle. Pieces of debris from the wrecked portable building lay on the ice alongside Cheryl's truck. Shards of paneling, broken glass, molding from the corner. The side was angled away from Wright by about thirty degrees.

Wright reached the door on the truck. He reached up and grabbed the steel of the mirror bracket. Pulled himself up onto the step.

Silver's truck started revving once more. Cheryl's truck jerked. One of Wright's feet slipped on the step.

The woman was just plain out of her mind. Collapsed across both trailers, the portable building had the two trucks locked together.

Perhaps her sheer determination would tear them apart.

Wright could hear the drive tires spinning on the ice. They needed one of those giant tow trucks to come and haul them out.

Wright yanked open the passenger door on Cheryl's truck.

Warm air rolled across him. It smelled of coffee and sandwiches. The interior was neat, with a couple of knickknacks on the dash. One might have been a St. Christopher's medal. Patron saint of travelers.

St. Christopher needed to come to the party about now and help out.

Wright climbed on across to the driver's seat.

The other truck's passenger window was about two feet way. With condensation and frost, he couldn't make out the woman too well. In a shadowy silhouette, she seemed to be leaning forward over the steering wheel.

As if pushing. Trying to manually break the truck free.

Wright slipped his legs between the driver's seat and the door. He tugged the handle. Opened the door slowly.

Right away the nose of the other truck rose at him. Loud and mechanical.

As if he was about to step into the engine room of a ship.

Wright kept the door close to his body. Foot down onto the first step. He slid backward and around the end of the door. He slipped it closed. Just to the first click.

Silver's truck revved again. The tires churned. They were chipping away at the ice. Turning a little section of the road to sludge.

The whole truck rumbled.

If he fell now, and the truck moved, forensics would be cleaning his body up with a spatula.

Wright reached across.

The vertical stainless steel exhaust belched and chugged. Wright gripped a handle set just behind the passenger's door. Like a towel rail, only set vertically. He'd used them many times when catching lifts aboard trucks.

Mostly in warmer climes.

Wright hauled himself across. The handle was slick. Cold moisture soaked into his gloves.

The woman was right there. Leaning forward. Working the gears. Tromping on the pedals.

Too focused to notice him.

Through the frosty haze of the window, Wright saw something dark on the passenger seat.

Could have been her gun. That little pistol she'd produced.

Easy enough for her to reach. She just had to snap it up and fire.

Wright opened the door.

CHAPTER THIRTY

The stink of diesel exhaust swirled around.

Wright launched himself into the cab.

Different to Cheryl's. Worn and grimy. A huge red thermal mug set in the central console.

He grabbed for the gun.

Not a gun. A hoagie sandwich.

A startled expression crossed the woman's face.

Momentarily.

Then she was in action.

Sliding down. Out of his path.

She dropped right into the footwell. Squirmed out of the way.

Wright grabbed for her. Got a hold of her hood.

She twisted away. Somehow squeezing around the gearstick and into the passenger's footwell. The advantage of being small and wiry.

The truck shook. Still running. Still in gear.

Without her lead foot on the gas, the truck was running at not much more than an idle. Tires spinning.

Wright lay across the two seats. Head near the steering wheel. Feet still just outside the open doorway.

Bad position.

"Give it up," he said.

"You don't understand!"

Wright was still moving. Squirming himself.

Trying to get up from the driver's seat. She was heading out through the open door.

Wright shunted his hands against the side of the driver's door. As if he was doing a clean and jerk. Whatever that move the weightlifters did when shoving enormous barbells above their heads.

The move shifted him back.

He kicked at the same time.

Caught her shoulder blade.

The woman yelped. Fell forward.

Vanished from sight.

Wright cursed.

CHAPTER THIRTY-ONE

In Silver's truck's cab, the CB radio gave a crackle. The engine droned on.

Wright bent at his waist.

Folded himself up. Swung around and forward out the door.

He grabbed at the vertical handle again. Right behind the door.

Swung out. Stumbled on the step.

The woman was below him. Legs lying on the ice. One hand gripping a lever on a supply locker in back of the cab. The kind of thing that stores ropes and straps, water and jacks and odd tools.

She looked up at Wright.

The wheels were still moving. Churning in the muddy, slushy hollows she'd created. Slow, but gradually working against the jam.

The portable building creaked and groaned.

The woman was holding on by just two fingers.

Slipping.

Wright stepped down. Kept hold of the vertical handle with his right hand. The steel was slippery. His hand jammed in right at the bottom.

She looked up at him. Face bleak. Terrified.

She couldn't have been more than twenty. The tires were just a couple of yards back from her legs.

The truck shuddered.

Wright stretched down for her. Couldn't quite reach. Not if he kept his grip on the handle.

The tires whined. Watery ice splashed around.

The portable building shifted. Another strap split and twanged.

Wright let go.

He stuck out his left boot. Got it onto the bottom step of Cheryl's truck.

Straddled between them.

He leaned left. Bent his left knee. Straightened, as if he was jumping.

Kicked himself back toward Silver's truck.

Bent his right knee. Grabbed low at the door frame.

The woman yelped. Holding on by her fingertips.

Wright whipped his left hand out. Grabbed her left wrist.

The truck shuddered again.

His right foot jerked off the step.

Something twinged in his right arm. His elbow made a terrible popping sound.

Wright held on.

His feet hit the ground.

Stumpy blocky numb things.

The truck was making slow headway.

The thing should have had a deadman's switch. If there was no one at the wheel, the engine shut off. At least dropped out of gear.

He should have shut off the ignition before following her out.

No sense in worrying about that now.

He dragged the woman back toward him. Up toward the cab. She was tiny. Light.

But he was exhausted. Numb and cold.

Why was he even doing this? She'd shot three people.

Maybe it was justice to simply let her fall back and risk the truck rolling on over her.

He was going to end up getting her to safety and falling back himself.

He kept pulling. Got her high enough that she was standing on the ice.

Kept pulling. Lifted her higher.

She came face to face with him. Stared right into his eyes.

"Thank you," she mouthed.

Even though he was the one who'd kicked her out of the truck.

"Climb," he said.

She did. Scrambled up and over him and into the cab.

Wright followed. He hauled the door closed behind him.

The truck jerked. Headed forward.

Broken free of its mooring. The portable building was breaking apart.

"Shut off the engine," Wright said, fully expecting her to point her gun at him and to hit the accelerator.

But she shut off the engine.

A sudden silence enveloped them.

"I shot Kev," she said into it. "I had to. I had to stop him."

"Keys," he said. "Wait here. You can tell me on the way north."

CHAPTER THIRTY-TWO

While Paul Silver got busy unhitching his truck from the trailer with its messed-up load, Wright and the woman got Hank and Green into Silver's cab. It was growing dark now, the distant sun fading off through the trees.

"You believe me?" the woman asked Wright. Her name was Gwen and she'd been trying to get away from this guy Kev for weeks.

"I believe you." Wright said. "But ultimately it will be a matter of ballistics and prints. C.S.I.s will come and take a look and see if they can piece together the crime scene."

"But you saw him shooting, didn't you?" Gwen said.

Wright had to shake his head. He'd heard shots and kept his head down.

Between getting Green and getting Hank, Gwen showed him Kev.

He was under Green's truck. Right in at the front axle.

A bullet hole in his forehead.

Just like the woman in the snowbound car.

Already Kev's skin had been growing gray and frosty. They left him there.

Crowded into Silver's truck's cab, they motored north. Silver worked the C.B., getting emergency services prepared for what was coming. They were an hour from Stinton, about the same amount of time it was going to take to get an ambulance helicopter from the hospital at a place called Kensington Lakes.

Green and Hank were laid out on the narrow bed behind the cab's seats. Not really even enough space for one person, but they had to manage it.

Hank's bullet graze wasn't so bad, but he'd hit his head coming down and had nasty scalp wound.

Wright had found a first aid kit in Cheryl's truck and used it supplement what they had from Green's truck. Silver had one too. Gloves, tape, bandages, saline, pads, disinfectant. They ran through the inventory pretty quick. It was a jam with Wright and Gwen in the back.

They focused on the work.

"We're getting your bedding real bloody back here," Gwen said.

Silver didn't reply. The truck's lights blazed through the fading day, showing the gloomy road ahead. The truck shook and rumbled. Going too fast. It felt light and loose, as if relieved to be free of the load.

"I came up a year back to be with Hank," Gwen said. "Sarah showed up a few days ago. She used to be with Hank, decided she wanted him back. But before she'd been with Hank, she'd been with Kev."

Green sucked in a deep breath. Murmured something.

Wright kept working. The feeling was coming back to his fingers. His feet tingled. The air was warm and dry.

He used one of the square pads to soak up more blood from Hank's scalp. It just kept bleeding, even taped down.

"I assume Kev shot her," Gwen said. "He could get kind of... nuts."

"And today?" Wright said.

"Me," Green said, barely audible. "Sarah and me were

together right after she was with Kev, before she was with Hank."

Green's eyes were teary. Or glassy. It could just be the injuries. Could be emotion.

"Regular soap opera, huh?" Silver said from up front.

"Just with guns," Gwen said. "I shot him. In the end. It was me. I'll go to jail."

"Self defense, I'm sure," Wright said. "Justifiable. He'd already shot three people."

"But you didn't see. Nobody saw."

"I saw," Green whispered.

"You were shot from behind," Wright said. "And you fell over the berm. You couldn't have seen a thing."

"Doesn't matter. That's what I'll testify."

Gwen looked at Wright, her face bleak. "I'll get the blame for it all," she whispered.

"I saw some too," Silver said. "Kev shooting. He always was a bad egg."

"You know him?"

"Everyone knows everyone." Silver cleared his throat. "Kind of. This one, Gwen, I don't know her."

She closed her eyes. Tightly.

Silver glanced back. "Huh," he said. "Well, maybe I do remember you. Didn't we have a game of pool at *Snooker's Bar* a few weeks back?"

Gwen said nothing.

"Yeah, we did," Silver said. "You told me you'd never shot a gun. Didn't know one end from the other."

Gwen's nostrils flared. She sighed.

"One end from the other is pretty important with guns," Silver said with a laugh.

Gwen nodded.

It didn't quite sit right. The cops would come and they would forensically examine the scene as best they could. They'd be able to determine the order of events.

Probably.

Wright wouldn't be any kind of witness. He'd seen Gwen with the rifle. Seen her desperate, crazed attempt to flee the scene.

But these people knew each other. Looked out for each other.

He would never know. And he would have to live with that.

But over his time, he'd seen plenty of things go wrong. People set up and sent down for crimes they hadn't done. People escaping charges on technicalities.

Good people making tiny mistakes that cost them everything. People defending themselves.

The bleeding on Hank's head seemed to have stopped.

Wright peeled off the gloves and balled them up. He shifted around through the gap and into the passenger seat.

Far ahead there was a vague glow on the horizon that might have been from Stinton.

"The road back there is blocked," Silver said.

"The cops will be there soon."

"Maybe."

"I thought you called it in?"

"I called for the chopper. I figured that, well--" he glanced over at Wright "--that we needed to get the story straight before I did that."

Wright glanced back at Gwen. She looked scared.

He'd kicked her out of the truck and she'd almost gone under the tires.

"How to do you work this?" Wright said, reaching up for the C.B. microphone.

"You're going to tell them it was me?" Gwen said.

"No," Wright said. "I'm going to tell them that the road is blocked. That there are three bodies. That's all."

"Thank you," she said.

"You're welcome."

Silver clicked a switch and told Wright to go ahead.

Wright spoke, got told to change channels, which Silver did

for him. A dispatcher came on, probably down in some warm office building in Toronto or Vancouver.

Wright explained the situation and got put through to local enforcement. He explained about the trucks and bodies and that they were ferrying the injured pair to Stinton

"Blocked road?" the woman cop said. She was in Harsavale, a town fifty miles south. "Bodies?"

"That's right. You need something to clear the road, and someone to take care of the scene. The bodies."

"Yes. Did you see it? You a witness?"

Wright glanced back at Gwen. Her eyes were closed. Lips moving. She might have been praying.

"No officer," Wright said into the microphone. "I really didn't see any of it."

"Well, then," the cop said. "You get those people to safety, we'll come up and take care of the rest. But stay in touch."

"Yep," Wright said. "I will."

He hung up the microphone.

"Nicely handled," Silver said, with a glance over. "Honest as you could be."

"I hope so," Wright said.

Gwen leaned forward and touched his shoulder.

"Thank you," she said.

"Of course. Keep an eye on those two. Tell me if they turn bad."

"Yes." She sounded lighter. More relaxed.

She wasn't in the clear yet, but as far as he could see, there was no reason to drop her in it. She would be okay.

Wright leaned back in the seat and stretched out.

Far, far in the distance, the lights of Stinton grew slowly brighter. And off to the right, through the trees, he thought he glimpsed the running lights of a helicopter.

Things would work out, in their own way.

AFTERWORD

Thanks for reading Cold Highway. I hope you enjoyed it as much as I enjoyed writing it. I do have a blast writing the Cole Wright books, both the stories and the novels, and in this case, a novella. I think Cold Highway is one of my personal favorites.

Feel free to drop by and say hi at seanmonaghan.com. I'd love to hear from you. I do occasional updates and drop in free fiction from time to time. When I can figure out a mailing list, and how to do giveaways I'll get that happening too.

It's pretty awesome these days with indie publishing that I can connect with readers.

Take care out there.

Sean

ACKNOWLEDGEMENT

I am grateful again to Vera Soroka for her helpful insights into an earlier version of this novella.

ABOUT THE AUTHOR

A frequent traveler from his home in New Zealand, Sean Monaghan has made it to twenty-six countries so far, all providing rich settings for his stories, which run the spectrum from thrillers to science fiction to literary. With visits to forty-nine U.S. and a couple of Canadian provinces, Sean likes to think he knows his way around.

An award-winner, Sean writes from a nook in the corner of his 110 year old home.

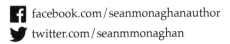

facebook.com/seanmonaghanauthor
twitter.com/seanmmonaghan

ALSO BY SEAN MONAGHAN

COLE WRIGHT THRILLERS

The Arrival

Measured Aggression

Hide Away

Slow Burn

Scorpion Bait

Zero Kills (December 2022)

COLE WRIGHT SHORT STORIES

Dark Fields

Schedule Interruption

The Forest Doesn't Care

The Handler

One Little Broken Leg

COLE WRIGHT NOVELLA

Cold Highway

CPSIA information can be obtained
at www.ICGtesting.com
Printed in the USA
LVHW050424081122
732583LV00004B/217